Clint Faraday
56
Road Kill

Clint gets a call from Rosario Puentes, police, to say there was a road kill found on the bridge near Chiriqui. Seeing he was in David, would he like to help the investigation?

"Road kill? So what?"

"He was a man named Ernesto Barco. He was popular. We don't know who would kill him or why. It doesn't look like it could have been a hit and run."

Oh. That kind of road kill.

Contents

About the author

CD Moulton has traveled extensively over much of the world both in the music business, where he was a rock guitarist, songwriter and arranger and in an import/export business. He has been everything from a bar owner to auto salvage (junkyard) manager, longshoreman to high steel worker, orchid grower to landscaper, tropical fish farmer to commercial fisherman. He started writing books in 1983 and has published more than 350 books as of January 1, 2023. His most popular books to date are about research with orchids, though much of his science fiction and fantasy work has proven popular. He wrote the CD Grimes, PI series, and the Det. Nick Storie series, Clint Faraday series, and many other works.

He now resides in Gualaca, Chiriqui, Panamá, where he writes books, plays music with friends, does research with orchids and medicinal plants. He has lately become involved in fighting for the rights of the indigenous people, who are among his closest friends, and in fighting the extreme corruption in the courts and police in Panamá.

He offers the free e-book, *Fading Paradise*, that explains what he has been through because of the corruption.

CD is the discoverer of the Chadam Protocol for curing cancer.

Facebook page Ambrosia peruviana for cancer.

Clint Faraday, PI, drove onto the careterra at Chiriqui where it met the Bocas road and pulled into the filling station. He saw several people he knew from cases in the area. This was close to David, where he was heading. He was there investigating what seemed to be a scheme by some politicians to steal a bit of the Indio land. There was a small bit of gold there. It was an old story where they took more and more land in little pieces.

Clint would see them exposed and there would be no stealing of land in the comarca.

Rosario Puentes, a cop he'd met in Panamá City, was there in the police truck. He greeted Clint warmly and said that he was head of investigations here at the National Police Station.

"It's an easy job, thanks to God! Chiriqui is a very tranquil town. There is little real crime, though I will miss the intense investigations we had in the city."

"There's nothing that most cops want more than that they aren't needed for that kind of thing," Clint replied.

"True! A dedicated cop wishes for nothing more than that he works himself to the point his job is unnecessary.

"It will never happen I fear, my friend. People will ever remain people. A percent of them are animals without morals or any sense of others.

"Why can't they look in a mirror, as do we, and ask themselves if this is what life is about? Is this what I wish to be my legacy?

"You are here because of that attempt by those four politicians in David trying to seize comarca land. They are sordid thieves and worse. They talk about their legacy to their children, but can't see what that legacy must be.

"I don't want my children and theirs to say, 'Papa or abuelo was a cheap crooked piece of shit! I'm so proud to be descended from such!'

"I'm, as you say in Florida, preaching to the choir!

"How is the family? Are you still enjoying this paradise place?"

"More than ever. I heard you're a father now. That why the sermon?"

He laughed. "It makes one think."

"Only those who are capable of thinking. I think you'll leave a legacy your descendants will be proud of."

"If I can simply leave one where they say I was

a decent person I will be content. Less and less are leaving that."

They chatted a bit longer, then Clint moved on toward David and his expected confrontation. He was fortunate his reputation was what it was. The people he was going to face down weren't known for gentility. They would have him killed in a minute – if they thought they could get away with it. It was what they were.

He remembered when there was a minor purge conducted by a group the corruption in the courts and police had hurt, cheating some of their entire life's savings or more. (*A Bloody Shame*) and thanked a god he didn't believe in for not letting him be one of those.

He went to the Pensión Costa Rica, got a room, talked a bit with Lee, the owner, and went to the Ciudad Judicial – with two reporter friends.

The four people he was supposed to see had an emergency come up. They were in Panamá City with no return date noted. Sorry, Old Top, and all that rot, eh, what?

Rojelio, from The Press, and Sonya, from TVN, smirked as they went out. They both immediately used their cellulars to ask where the four were. It seems they were all at the estate of one of them in Veraguas.

It was reported in a short note on TV and in the

morning edition of the newspaper exactly what Clint was there for and exactly what they were told and exactly what they knew.

"Mr. Faraday, the very well-known advocate for people's rights and always in the forefront in fighting corruption in Panamá, states that these people are acting in a very unethical, in even a criminal manner. The people must act to stop this travesty. Panamá is too fine a place for this kind of thing to be longer allowed. Demand of your legislators that this *stops*! Now!"

Clint grinned. They would have to reply fast and they would have to back down.

Sure enough! Ten minutes later Guerra, the head of the scheme, came on a special report to cry that it was only one part of an investigation of a problem where the needs of the country must come before the needs of a few individuals. They had *already* rejected the plan as not being feasible! That was why they were meeting at his home!

"I see," Juliana, the reporter, replied. "You came here to your estate in Veraguas at the time you had a fixed appointment with Mr. Faraday to discuss what you would have told him if you'd kept that appointment?"

"Er, um."

"Back to you, Sandra."

Clint laughed. He bought a round of beers for the people who were watching the report with him and went back to the Costa Rica to sack out. He'd accomplished what he came to accomplish without having a nasty face-to-face confrontation. As they say, "His reputation had preceded him."

Hi cel brought him awake at four thirty in the morning, about the time he usually got up. He answered it to hear Sario (Rosario Puentes) say there had been a case of road kill on the bridge near Chiriqui. Maybe he would like to help with the investigation?

"Road kill? So what?"

"He was a man named Ernesto Barco. He was popular. We don't know who would kill him or why. It doesn't look like it could have been a hit and run."

Oh. That kind of road kill.

"I'm done here. I'll come right away. About forty five minutes. I'll get breakfast there."

"I'll be at the restaurant just past – before, from that direction – the bombas."

"I'd say it was a hit and run, but not the kind where somebody hits someone and panics and runs. Someone who purposefully hit someone, threw the body off the bridge, and ran!" Sario said, showing Clint the pictures of the scene on his digital camera.

"Yes. The body has been definitely described as probable death from vehicular causes?" (That was how the Spanish translated.)

"Yes. From vehicular attack, though it is not the final analysis. Dr. Hernandez says he has great reservations, but the body was hit on the road and dropped off the bridge onto rocks twelve meters below. There is little water in the river this time of the year."

"I saw that on my way in. There's some water shortage in David. IDAAN says they need to dam all the rivers around to be able to supply enough, which will destroy the ecology of the area. You can't help but note that the aqueduct is full, hmm?"

"The aqueduct was to guarantee the water. They built it, now they need more. They just want more power.

"No politics now. We can agree on what they are later.

"Dr. Hernadez says it appears as though Barco was hit with a piece of pipe or something that would have killed him. He wants to be able to show that officially before he makes it his report. He's smart not to stick his head on the block unless he can pretty well prove what he says."

"So. That's also politics? What was Barco into? You said he was popular."

"He was an officer at Frontera. He had charges brought against some other border officers for corruption. There is now an investigation. The investigation is based on his testimony.

"DUH!"

"Meaning we won't get anywhere with our own investigation and theirs will stop."

"If it's 'we,' that is true. If it is Clint Faraday acting because he stated that the people must rise up and put an end to this? Will that give them pause, do you think?"

"You give me far too much credit, but I'll give it a try.

"I don't suppose there's a chance we can get a copy of the charges?"

"No. Other department. Not authorized."

"Have you been to his house?"

"Only to tell the widow and son of the death. They were fatalistic. Paulo said they tried to tell him he was, what do you say? Signing his own death warrant?"

"Will they let me into the house to look for things?"

"You are a special police agent. I have a copy of those papers. You can go there and may enter. I can't."

"Show me the house. I'll see if maybe he left us something to go on.

"There is a fifty percent of a chance that the killer will think the fact I may not enter and that the family are afraid will mean no one will look there. The least is that they will think there is time."

They took Clint's car. Sario showed Clint an average house in an average neighborhood. It was clean and neat and had some gardening. A young man was by the door, apparently arguing with an older man.

Clint pulled into the parking area in front of the house and went to the door. He had the papers from his glove case that said he was authorized for special investigation by the National Police and could enter any property with cause.

"Berto Barco?" he asked of the younger man.

"Yes."

He handed him the paper. "There is evidence that your father was murdered. He brought about an investigation. I have cause. I will appreciate it if you will show me where Mr. Barco's items are. I would not wish to interfere with the rights of anyone else."

"I am here to do the investigation!" the older man snapped.

"You are?"

"Carlos Pencero."

"Show me your authorization to enter a domicile papers, Mr. Pencero."

"I don't need authorization papers! I represent the National Police!"

"Yes, you do. What is your department? Why are you here without notification of our offices?"

"Er, I'm with immigration. Frontera. Aduana."

"Then you have no authorization and there is no implied authorization, Mr. Pencero. That is noted and explanations will be demanded or I will bring charges against *you*!"

"May I speak with you in private?"

"No. I believe in the transparency laws."

"I am here because of the charges Barco has brought."

"I don't doubt that! Which side?"

Pencero stared for a few seconds, then turned and walked away. Sario was standing by the gate.

He stopped and said something. Sario said, just loud enough to be heard, "He has authorization from the main offices. What am I supposed to do? Why come to me? *He* is the superior officer here!"

Sario turned to grin at Clint as Pencero stomped toward his car. A new BMW.

"Nice car for a cop to be driving, huh?" Clint asked Berto, who grinned and said to come on in. He waved for Sario to come.

"You don't mean you will actually try to avenge my father's murder?"

"No. We will do everything in our power to bring his killers to justice," Sario answered. "I think you will have heard of Clint Faraday and his success rate!"

"You are Clint Faraday?! I begin to have hope!"

They went in to a small interior room, actually an expanded and converted closet that had a desk and computer and file cabinet inside.

"I would not have let him know of this room, had he entered," Berto declared. "Mother and I already made plans. If they come in she will open the door and put in the mop and broom, like it is a closet for cleaning tools. She would do that while they were in front and could not see inside. She would then tell me we need Clorox and go into the kitchen. I would show them Mother and Father's room and tell them they could not go anywhere else. There is a copy of the charges in the drawer there, which is what they would want. They would take it and go."

"Good plan!" Sario said. "You could also tell them your father did not keep those things here."

"I would tell them he gave all the papers I ever saw to the man from Panamá City, the one from the Junta Nacional or whatever they call it."

"They would feel safe with that. Those national committees never seem to do anything," Clint said.

"They do something! They draw a big salary and have the bribes to add!" Berto said with a grimace. "The government agencies are corrupt through to the center. It is the way things are done here. It is why, I agree with Mr. Faraday about this, Panamá has a bad reputation in the world. From outside they can't see it is only a few. A corrupt animal is appointed or elected to head some office and he will only hire those he can get a cut from. It is why I have faint hope you will be able to solve this."

"I'll solve it," Clint promised. "The problem will be getting the courts to act."

"They won't, except with great publicity," Sario added. "Clint has an ability to garner publicity, as Guerra and companions discovered."

"I saw the television. I had some hope he would

try to explain to Juliana that she had misunderstood or something. He did have the intelligence to just walk away. She is known to pursue such ridiculous statements by officials with great determination. He could not win. She would have shown him for more of a fool than she did!"

Clint asked permission to search the computer. Berto said he didn't need permission, but he certainly had it!

He sat at the computer and booted. He went directly to MS-DOS to read the registry. There was a section of the hard drive that was isolated and needed a code to enter.

"Berto, did your father ever tell you how to get into the partitioned section?"

"I-f-f-l-e-s-k-e-l-b-u-t-i-n-c."

"Sheesh!" He tried it on the login. It brought up another file that needed a code.

"B-e-a-t-l-e-b-a-u-m."

He had a long note pad document. It pretty much described exactly what was going on at the border. It said the pictures were numbered and gave a list of times, dates, names, licence plate numbers, make and model and whatever else was needed for the particular picture.

There was then a list of fifty three pictures.

"Big problem! There aren't any pictures!" Clint cried.

Berto grinned and took a memory stick from under the monitor base. Clint plugged it in and had the pictures, plus the document, plus several other things.

"Father felt he would be arrested on some false charge. I was to give the memory stick to anyone I could trust and allow them to try to open the file on the computer. If I didn't trust you, there would be no mention of the stick and I wouldn't know how to access the computer section.

"Mother and I were very much afraid that they would torture or kill him. We made the plan for if they did. He would not stop. He said that if they killed him he would die an honorable man. They would forfeit any hope to ever do the same. He always taught me that there are things in life that a person must not even consider if he wished for a good afterlife.

"He was religious. Mother is some. I'm not very much. If the god of the church is the real one, Father is in a far better place. We have that consolation."

Clint nodded. He could see that everything on the computer was on that memory stick. He asked permission to format the hard drive.

"If that ass or any other comes, you can tell them I went to the comp and tried something to get into a secret file and the computer then was erased. I may not have used the right code and there might have been something your father put there to be sure no one who wasn't authorized could read anything.

"When I leave I'll swear a lot. You can tell them I was swearing when I left without lying."

"I do not mind lying to such as them. It will ease Mother's mind to be able to truthfully say such. She will actually hear you swearing when you leave. She doesn't understand much English, though she knows that certain hard words are maldiciones."

Clint gave the computer orders to government format the hard drive. They waited more than twenty minutes for it to finish, then Clint and Sario left. The mother was by the front door. Sario wished her a very pleasant day. Clint was steadily swearing at anything said. Berto smirked at his mother and shrugged.

"So. You gave it to them and this is so I will be able to say honestly that they were very angry when they left and that Mr. Faraday was as much as rude to me." She patted Sario's hand and smiled.

"Go with God," she added.

Clint left Sario at the station and took the memory stick with him to the Costa Rica. He had his personal laptop there and could use a special program to make notes as he went.

First was an explanation. It started when there were claims of bribe-taking by some of the border guards. One guard was killed in David in a very suspicious manner and the police didn't bother to investigate the murder. Barco began his own investigation using equipment he bought himself to get photographs and sound evidence. He investigated for three months and found the worst of the offenders, though the few who were not engaged in the bribes and favors were a very small minority.

Clint could see, considering what he'd learned about the courts and special cops such as the border aduana guards, that this one as much as set himself up to be killed. He had to know that he wouldn't survive long enough to testify against those officials at that level.

He made out a complete explanation of the evidence and put it in a file that would bring the whole thing up much as it would bring up a high-end catalogue. Pictures with explanations in chronological order.

He sat back to think, then called Sario. "Where are the vehicles used by the border guard kept when they're in this area?"

"David. Behind the judicial. Why?"

"That BMW wasn't damaged. Your pictures show he was hit by a car or truck, even if he was already dead. I can find which one. It will tie their asses to a fence post!"

"Clint, a little mercy here! Please don't do that."

Clint laughed and gave the phone the finger. He went out to his car and headed for the Ciudad Judicial. He caused a bit of a panic when he demanded to inspect the vehicles in the compound. They tried to refuse, he called Panamá City, who told them to obstruct a special corruption official was a crime in itself. The name of the person who caused that obstruction would be noted and explanation would be demanded.

"I'm just some guy who's supposed to look after the lot! They said nobody was authorized to be on the lot without a pass they give them! This officer doesn't have one!"

"He has papers from here that say he can go anywhere at anytime for any reason. Those papers supercede any silly pass requirement. You are noted and will file a reason with this office at Officer Faraday's demand."

"Oh, God!"

"Tell me who gave that order and I'll forget it," Clint suggested.

"But ... you don't understand what they'll do!"

"Well, then you will tell me who it wasn't if I ask."

"That will work. I won't say a name."

"Jorge Martin."

"No."

"Luis Comacho."

"No."

"Carlos Pencero."

"It's windy today."

"Well, if you won't tell me, you won't tell me. I'll file charges for non-cooperation and forget to pursue them, okay?"

"Thanks. I really don't want to do this, but I have a wife and baby. I need the work.

"I should go in and tell them you have papers and Panamá City is on my ass?"

"Might be a good idea. Tell them I'm going to charge you with obstruction and they have to stop the charges. Panamá City said I had to do that."

Clint went into the lot and the gateman headed for the offices at almost a run.

Clint found a truck with some damage to the

right headlight area. There was a broken signal light housing. There was a slight stain on the plastic. It would prove to be blood. If it was Barco's, they had no way out.

He took careful pictures and evidence samples and headed for his car. He was getting in when he heard a scraping sound from behind the trash cans by the building. He saw (he had exceptional peripheral vision) a hand with a pistol move around a steel barrel and point toward him. He dropped and a shot went a few inches over his head. He rolled to the close car and crawled quickly around behind. He got to his feet and went around the other side of the car in time to see the back of a person with a loose blue jean jacket and a ski mask running around the back of the building.

He thought *I'm getting too old for this shit!* and ran for the building and through. The guard at the front started after him. He couldn't get to the back door without going down a hall full of people. He wouldn't have a chance of seeing anything anyhow.

He asked a woman sitting in a chair across from an office if anyone came through the hall from the rear. Someone wearing a blue jean jacket.

"No. Only the woman from the records."

He thanked her and went back to the officer

chasing him to report what had happened and to show him the papers.

"You are supposed to stop and show the papers at the desk! I am going to arrest you!"

"Okay."

"Er, what?"

"You're going to arrest me. That's the fastest way for me to see the people I have to see, I think! Good idea!"

"Ah, that is, perhaps we should calm down. We must not get too upset over a minor infraction."

"Oh, no! It's your job to arrest me! It's what you're paid to do!"

"Well, it's a special circumstance. We can just forget it!"

"But that isn't your decision to make."

"The papers make it very plain that I'm not to interfere with you in any way. I will not arrest you."

"I see. If you do something that gets me directly to them, you pay the price."

"I really must get back to the front. My wife and son and daughter will be coming here from the school."

"Can any of them see you now?"

"Yes sir. That's the way it is. Please check with the guard in the future to avoid any problems."

"Can they hear us?"

"I really can't say. Have a nice day!" He walked back toward the front.

So. Even the local building security guard is being intimidated. They threaten the family.

They were going to regret having Clint Faraday after their asses! Bitterly! Promise!

He headed for his car. On the way around the building he considered: The only way out from back there was through that gate or through that back door. No one came in that back door.

There were three people standing by his car. They heard the shot and saw him run into the building.

"Has anyone come from the back lot since I left?"

"No."

"You might be in danger if you're this close to me. He might try another shot."

They looked nervous and moved away a bit. Clint thought, then got his own Glock from the car and headed for the gate. There was no one back there. He went to the back door and opened it to find the woman still sitting there. He asked if anyone came through.

No.

He went back and around the fence. There was a spot against the building where the fence was cut. It was behind a large croton and couldn't be seen from anywhere more than a few feet away. He could have gone through and into the side parking lot, then to the road and away.

He went back to the trash barrels and looked around carefully. He found a .40 caliber casing. He picked it up with tweezers and studied it. He printed it to find what appeared to be a thumb on one side and an index finger on the other.

"Hey, Clyde! You didn't wear gloves when you loaded that thing?

"Big mistake!"

He fished out an envelope and dropped in the casing and the print strip. Unless the shooter was from another country and in Panamá illegally he would know who loaded the pistol in an hour.

Knowing who loaded the pistol wouldn't prove anything in a court that was paid not to find evidence. It would tell Clint who to look for.

He wouldn't use the legal system. That would be a dead end road. The case was decided and closed before it was brought up. The corrupt courts were the biggest thorn in the side of Panamanian investment. Panamá's reputation worldwide was terrible because of it.

Deservedly so.

This case was like the corruption game in a way or two. If you were using the corruption, you had to know to go to the top or nothing would ever happen other than layer on layer of bribes. Go for the top man.

He was going to do that here. His problem was to find who was the top man – or woman. He would then have to get some kind of proof that would hold up to public exposure. It was certain as sunset that nothing else would work.

Clint headed for his car, then went to Chiriqui as fast as he safely could. He took the print strips to Sario to ask that they be checked quietly. No one needed to know he was looking for anyone specific.

"The prints are from?"

"A shell casing from a bullet that was fired at me." He gave a quick rundown about what had happened.

"I'm going back to town as soon as I can get into a disguise. I'll take the Chiriqui – David bus. I won't look much like me. If you get any calls, 'Clicker' Diaz is someone you keep an eye on the rare times he's in the area. You've never been able to tag him for anything yet, but bad things happen when he's around.

"You didn't know he was in Chiriqui. He might have just come from Colón or Panamá City and changed buses in Chiriqui. I'll get Sergio and Naldo to back up a story."

"Sergio? He's head of investigation of violence in the academy. Naldo is retiring soon. He's in Chitre."

"Yeah. Not here, so the story might not be a cover, huh? I'll add one more, but that's not one you would be concerned with. It's also one that would explain me being here to change buses. It's one no one can check on very well."

He went to his car and to a friend's place in Higueron. He made the calls to Sergio and Naldo, two people who were very high-ranking police he had worked with over the years. The next was to Silvio in Soloy. That was in the comarca and there wouldn't be any way to check on it.

The person who walked away from Enrique's place later was a slightly seedy-looking man in his late forties or early fifties. He had a full beard and a scar across the cheek above the beard. He had bushy eyebrows and a very slight hitch to his step. He was wearing black jeans and a black and silver Metalica tee shirt. He was wearing cowboy boots and one hand had a glove with no finger. He had a way of looking at you that was more than a little scary. His wallet was in his right rear pocket and had a sliver chain that was attached to his fancy leather belt with the big silver and turquoise buckle. There were ten hundred dollar bills in the wallet, along with a few twenties and tens. He was slender, but powerful.

He caught the Gualaca bus at the bombas and sat next to a fat older woman who was flirting with several men. She did *not* try to flirt with him! She got very quiet when he sat. It was one of the only two seats available. The other had a woman with two small children. Most would avoid it until there was no choice.

The driver turned the radio a bit louder when they were on the carretera. The man was heard to mutter, "Goddamned fucking salsa shit!"

It was an uncomfortable ride for the people close into David. They didn't quite know why, but this was one scary dude!

The man got off across from the Cattán Clinic and walked up toward the markets. He didn't go near the terminal. He went into a little bar and ordered a seco and coke. There were two Indios and the barmaid, who had to write on a pad at the other end of the bar all of a sudden.

When she was out of hearing Clint spoke to the

Indios in dialect for a few minutes, then left with the plastic cup of seco and coke in his hand. He stopped just outside and heard the barmaid say, "El es maldito! Cuidado! Hay mieda!"

One of the Indios said, "He was in Soloy. They made him leave."

Good! That would get around. His Indio friends would see to it!

He went on and into another bar where a lot of what they called "Mafia" hung out. He listened to the chatter. These weren't the type to be afraid of anyone, but they were suddenly cautious about this cold stranger. He didn't mix. It somehow seemed plain that he wasn't the mixing type.

After a few minutes he went to sit near the door at a small table. He didn't speak to anyone or do anything. Conversation soon went back to the normal bar chatter. He heard names that wouldn't mean anything to him and what he was working on. These types were name-droppers.

A big black man he'd seen in Bocas soon came in. Changuinola. Big mouth. Tried to be a big-shot. The type who threw names around like he was a close friend, but they were people he'd never met and who wouldn't have anything to do with him. Those people didn't like anyone around who had diarrhea of the mouth. He liked to be called "Spike" – but they called him Bennie.

He would give Clint – or "Clicker" – what he wanted!

"You!" Clint said in English when he walked by with his Chivas on the rocks.

"Me? What?"

"I saw you in Changuinola. I never forget a face. Maybe in Frontera, once. With that Pencero mouthy piece of shit."

"Carlos? In Changuinola? He has power."

"Sixola, maybe in ... no. Frontera. With that sneaky asshole. The one who says he can call in the Mexican Mafia with a phone call."

"DelaCruz? He can! I was with him once when he did. In San Miguelito. Some Rusos who were giving him shit."

"Yeah, right! You're the one who's full of shit! Nobody, including the Mex, are about to start anything with Ivan and Vasily Armakov!"

"Uh, it wasn't them. It was someone named, uh, Smirnof, I think."

"Sarnov? The same's true as with Vasily and Ivan."

"Uh, I'm not sure. It sounded that way to me."

"Yeah. DelaCruz is dug in at Dolega, last I heard. He ain't hiding his slimy ass because he's such a big bad piece of shit!"

"He's moved to San Antonio – the urbanization. Got a place for eight hundred grand. Cash."

"Well, I'll be looking for work soon. I'll go through what I have in a month. Not for that crud!"

"What kind of work."

"Things."

"Armakov will recommend you?" He said it with a slight sneer. He had been sizing Clint up and thought he could take him. Clint hid a smirk.

"Vasily? Recommend someone? You're that stupid?

"Sarnov might say to talk to me about things. I wouldn't ask for any recommendation from anyone. Keep a low profile and live. Run your stupid fucking mouth like you and be sure you keep your affairs in order. You're gonna take the big dive before you're thirty."

"Fuck you, gringo! You don't scare me! Your type are a dime a dozen!"

"How original. Get out of my face or I'll get you out of it, capiche?" He hissed that.

Bennie dropped his drink and grabbed for Clint's shirt. The next thing he knew he was on the floor staring at the holes in the ceiling, such as it was.

"Anybody asks you what happened to your face you tell them Clicker didn't like it and changed it for you, wimp!"

"My face? Happened to my face? What...?"

"Like this!" Clint kicked a glancing blow against

the side of his face. The heel of the riding boot tore a wide strip, which gushed blood.

"Now you have something to show what a big bad motherfucking piece of mouthy shit you are!"

Clint smiled what looked more like a sour grimace at the several people standing around and walked out.

He now had the name he wanted. DelaCruz. He could be sure everyone there would know he was called "Clicker." One of those people was Jorge, one of the Indios from the place before. He gave Clint a quick grin.

He went on toward the parque. People would go to almost extremes to not be in his way on the sidewalk. He didn't seem to notice. He went into the Multi-Café and had a meal, then went over to the Occidental Hotel, where he was told they had no rooms available. Same at the Iris. Wonder why!

His phone rang. "Clint? This is Silvio. Someone called. I told them you were not welcome on the comarca and would be most unwise to try to come here again."

"Thanks, Silvio. I need all the negative publicity I can get. I've found one name. DelaCruz."

"I have not heard it."

They chatted a little more and Clint went to the Puerto del Sol. No rooms. Sheesh! Same at the

Nacional.

He ended up at the hotel in the casino in San Mateo. He knew they wouldn't even notice he was an obvious hired killer type. There were others there like him.

Now to wait until he had one other small bit of information, then bring this to a head.

He laid back on the bed. His phone buzzed. It was Sario. "Nacio Benson. Zonie. Sixteen de Diciembre. Pedrigal."

"Thanks." He wouldn't say more. Sario knew he might be in a place where he dare not talk. It was altogether possible that room was bugged.

So. The one who shot at him was right there close. He didn't need anything from him, but it would be a good idea to get him off the streets. That would take five minutes!

Okay. Get him to mention DelaCruz or whoever he was using to contact people.

He soon got up and went outside, stood there thinking, then grabbed a passing bus to ride downtown. He caught the 16 de diciembre bus and rode to Pedrigal. He got off the bus at the road by the library that led to the worst part of the suburb and walked down the street. People avoided him. It was a section known for drug dealers and general hoods.

An attractive if obvious girl came by. He stopped

and asked where he could find Nacio. She said she
didn't know any Nacio.

"Okay. If you do, hope to Hell I never find out
you do."

"Uh, what does he look like? We don't know
many people by their real name here."

"Tall, thin, Zonie."

"Beegee? Sings like Andy Gibbs?"

"Could be."

"Second corner. Left. Third house on the left.
Two white columns. Likes guns. Careful!"

"He already tried to shoot me. Tends to piss me
off."

She giggled. "You gonna kill him?"

"Might."

"Fuck him first. Way he hates gays, serve him
right."

"I don't fuck guys. I don't care if anyone else
does. Both get what they want? Good for them.
Leave me out of it. Got gay friends. Who gives a
fuck?"

"Them. And get. You're fun. You like women,
I'm a woman?"

"When I don't have business."

"I'll be waiting!"

Clint went on to the house. He stood outside and yelled, "Nacio! Come out here! Now!"

The door opened and a sexy girl said he wasn't there. He went to the China.

Shit! He got off the bus right there! If Nacio saw him ... he wouldn't know who he was. He would know Clint Faraday, not Clicker Diaz.

The girl might tell him someone was looking for him.

He went back to the China and asked who Beegee was. The owner said he left about five minutes before. Took a cab for David.

"That one has money for cabs?"

"Sixty cents going to David. Three dollars from except at the stand. It's sixty from there."

He knew that, of course, but they would remember the hard, cold man who didn't know anything about the buses or cabs.

He thought a minute, smirked to himself and waved at a passing taxi. He rode to the main road and got out.

If Nacio's type was going somewhere other than local where everyone knew him he wouldn't do it from a spot anyone would notice. He would do what Clint did to make people think he'd left. If someone was looking for him he wouldn't want to be without his pistol!

Clint walked back to the corner just before the China, then walked a block up and came back to the street where he could watch who went into the suburb. The girl he'd talked to earlier was walking back up the street.

He waited. About fifteen minutes later the bus came by. A man got off at the China and went inside, then came to start walking up the street.

Clint went carefully out and came up behind the man.

"Beegee?"

He turned. His eyes started darting all around. There was a look of almost terror on his face.

"Don't run. I'm not going to kill you. If you had hit Faraday, I'd already have you in pieces all over the campo. You don't have a personal gripe with this. I doubt you've ever seen Faraday up close.

"Give me a name. If it checks out, you probably won't ever see me again. If it doesn't, you will.

"Believe me, you don't want to see me again if you've lied."

"They'll kill me!"

"They won't know it was you who gave me the

name."

He thought for a minute. He licked his lips and looked around, but there was no one closer than three blocks.

"Mancinni. I never said nothin' to you! You asked me about ... about Berto Arauz,! Okay?"

"Okay. If it checks out." Clint turned and went back to get a cab at the China.

"Ah! Beegee came back and went home," the owner said. That told Clint he hadn't been seen talking to Nacio.

"I saw him. He wasn't the one I was looking for. A wasted morning. Part of life."

A cab came by and he waved for it and left.

He had expected to hear the name, "DelaCruz." Instead, he heard, "Mancinni."

Mancinni was probably a gofer for DelaCruz – like Pencero.

Was DelaCruz top or was he second level? He wouldn't be lower than that.

Clint went into David and went through the phone book. It had a few DelaCruz listed.

Mancinni was second to – no! DelaCruz was second! Mancinni and Pencero were probably third level.

Find who Mancinni was and work up. He'd worked up from Nacio to Mancinni. He already knew DelaCruz was someone he would have to find and watch. Mancinni was a buffer. DelaCruz didn't know Clint had his name. Anyone was supposed to be able to trace to Mancinni, who was probably just a semi-mobster with delusions. He was, like Pencero, positioned to be the goat.

Mancinni would be easy to find. That was his value.

So. Find him. That was something that could backfire on them.

He called Sario. "Mancinni?"

"Yee! Mancinni! Arlo Mancinni?"

"Give."

"A real sleazy type of wannabe. He gets away with all kinds of things by bribing the courts and police in David. He has to have some higher connections or he would have been gone years ago. Runs some empeños and such. Launders money. Got started doing that for the cartels.

"There's no way he's the boss, Clint. He's a puppet."

"He's a goat. So in Pencero.

"DelaCruz?"

"Much bigger. Hires out so stays clean so far as we're supposed to know. Owns two judges and several really big police contacts. A lawyer, but doesn't practice. Has one Hell of a lot of money he couldn't explain if there was a way to question it that the judges haven't already closed. He could be the jefe of the whole thing. If he's involved, I wouldn't blink if he is jefe of jefes."

"He's not. He's level two."

"Who's one?"

"That's what I have to learn. There won't be a way to connect anyone unless and until we can put them together. I'll have to know where DelaCruz goes on social occasions. He'll have it rigged to where any contact looks like a chance meeting at a party or somewhere."

"He owns a very fancy restaurant. He goes there every night and most noons. Golden Gourmet on the CPA west of David. Known mostly by the very wealthy.

"Clint, maybe we can do something that would cause someone to have to contact him?"

"I was thinking along those lines.

"Sario, I think this is something ... DelaCruz isn't the top of this. He might be on other things. Someone is using him, probably for a cut. His type is always looking for another little place to take in a few more dollars.

"I'm going to have to use another disguise and we can cause whoever it is we're after to contact him. I'll try to be there to see who it is. I think just the fact they're there will prove what needs proving. I have a feeling that knowing who answers all the major questions.

"Sario, you noted Pencero was exceeding his authority by going to Barco's house. Maybe you can haul him in for questioning and can bring charges that would mean we have a lever. He can be forced to give us the head of the scheme."

"And the head of the scheme will then have to contact DelaCruz to have the judge throw out all charges to stop us from knowing who the head is. To do that they have to contact him quickly. If Pencero is questioned this afternoon and is to remain in carcel tonight it will be necessary for him to be contacted tonight."

"You got it!" They made their plans. Sario was having Pencero watched from the first and could have him picked up immediately.

"Clint, maybe he'll panic and make the mistake of calling his boss right them? We will have the number?"

"We can hope, but I think he'll have someone who will automatically contact someone else."

Clint went to Higueron for his car. He came out looking far different.

The very expensively clad handsome dark man with a silverheaded cane thanked the obviously wealthy woman who dropped him off in front of the Golden Gourmet. The valet came to park the Rolls Royce, but she said she was just showing her good friend from Madrid where the place was and drove off.

"Very kind and amiable woman," Clint said. "I am Ramón Ramirez. I believe Sra. Velasquez has made reservation?"

"You will have to talk with the reception desk about that. I just park cars. You're from Madrid?"

"Yes. My family is there. I will wish to relocate. Madrid is a bit too ocupado and buioso for my tastes anymore.

"We all get older and less adaptable."

He adjusted the $20,000 tie tack and went into the vestibule to the desk. He had a choice table next to the owner's private table. A beautiful woman came to hand him a menu. She asked if he would like to order wine. He said that was his usual procedure, and thanked her.

The wine steward came with a list.

"Hmm. Madeira Rio Janos, tinta, nineteen sixty two was quite acceptable. I will be dining on the beef bourguignonne, I believe. Rio Janos has a nice subtle fruity aftertaste. It blends well with the burgundy used in the meal.

"Yes. A split, if you will?"

He nodded and went to the wine rack. The wine was served at room temperature, but the steward asked if he preferred it chilled.

"Rio Janos? No! Of course not!"

The steward opened the bottle and moved to pour over the cork. Clint said, "Stop!

"I'm very sorry, but you do not have much experience with good wines I can see. You open the bottle and let it sit for five minutes to breath, then decant a bit over the cork. It will not smell correctly until the acid fumes are evaporated."

"I see. I only do what I'm told. I don't know about wine except that some are good and some aren't. You're the first in two years here who told me anything like that. The people here wouldn't notice if I poured Clos, I think. Most of them."

"Clos?"

"A boxed cheap wine from the almacen."

Clint laughed. "It is too true in too many places. A person will try to impress others by buying a split of three hundred dollar wine who would not know it was different from a three dollar wine.

"My good man, you are honest. I like that!" He opened a wallet that had a wad of hundreds to choke a horse, as the saying goes. He handed him a hundred dollar bill.

"Jesús Cristo! I never got more than ten dollars for a tip before!"

"And that from a man who was with a fancy puta he was trying to impress?"

The steward gave him a thumb up and a wink. "You're alright! Most of these pretenders are assholes ... I'm sorry. If my boss heard me talking to a customer like this I'd be looking for another job without recommendation!

"I know you really are sophisticated. It's the pretenders who are so high-and-mighty and snobs of the worst kind. You're just some guy who's nice and happens to have money.

"I'll put that you got some of the Merlot. It's just fifteen dollars a bottle. All of it was from a hijack – but I didn't tell you that."

"I make no protest about paying a reasonable price for a fine wine. It is of no concern how it was obtained. I don't just happen to have money, I worked for forty years to earn it.

"I would only protest if it were not the wine on the label."

"I'll bet you can tell from a sniff!" He poured a little of the wine over the cork and presented it. Clint smelled it and noted the correct odor. He took the glass it was poured over and tasted it.

"It is the correct wine for the label. Thank you, my good man."

The steward stiffened, winked and said, "If there is any request, please signal to me and it will be promptly handled." He pointed to a man who came in and toward the table and mouthed, "Jefe!"

"Thank you. That will be all. Please send the hostess to receive my order."

The man came to the big table next to Clint and nodded. Clint returned the nod. The hostess came to take his order, then went to the boss to whisper to him for a moment. She went on and the man came over.

"Sr. Ramirez? From Madrid? I am called Felix DelaCruz. My parents were from Madrid. My father. Mother was from right here in David.

"You are here on holiday or business?

"If it is not my concern, please say so. I do tend to pry. I won't be insulted."

"Please join me," Clint replied. "I am called Razo. Don't ask me why.

"I am seeking a place to retire. I find Madrid too busy anymore. My sons can take the banks. I have no need of money more than I have. The prices here would allow me to live in great luxury from the interest.

"I once felt I would like to own a restaurant if only because I could get the better food I prefer, prepared as I prefer.

"Silly, youthful pipe dreams. I would fail as a restauranteur in a month simply *because* I would demand things my way, not the way others prefer. It is a failing of many. I can see you have made success of the business. I commend you."

"My problem is finding qualified personnel. I see you know wine so would know in a second that my steward has no qualification as a wine steward."

"Yes. But he is of very good personality and does not take offense when I tell him to allow a fine wine to breathe before pouring the cork. He said, in a confidential tone, that many of the people who come here wouldn't know if he was pouring a fine wine like this or, what did he call it? Clos? From a box?

"That is refreshing and far overrides that he is not sophisticated in his work. It is a wise choice to employ such a personable person.

"I have always stated in the banking business that a wise manager knows to hire someone who knows a thing that he doesn't. That would possibly be as much as impossible here. No one is very sophisticated in fine wines, thus hiring a personable man who wishes to learn is wise management."

"Thank you. You have much the same outlook on these things as do I.

"I wish you bon appetite! I see my date is here. I will not intrude on your meal further." He shook hands and walked away.

Clint ate the truly delicious six hundred dollar meal and had the valet call a taxi for him.

He had taken several pictures of the two women who came to sit with DelaCruz with his Blackberry. One came about twenty minutes after the first. Clint was sure one of them would be who he wanted to know about.

He stood close by the reservations stand while waiting for the taxi. The hostess went to seat a couple and he quickly glanced over the list. Two names were pencilled in. L. Nuestras and Y. Chirenas.

"I'll be damned!" Clint muttered.

Then the taxi came to take him to the Ciudad de David Hotel.

Now to see if they were working with DelaCruz or were just using him.

Clint called Sario, who said for him to come to Chiriqui as soon as possible. He might have some more answers for him. There were two officers from the fiscalia there trying to make him release Pencero into their custody.

"I told them you had certification from the main offices in Panamá City that said only you could allow his release or someone with an authority issued by the president. I am trying to contact you. Here comes Nuñez now, so make it sound like I just contacted you. I'll put it on speaker."

"I'll be there in half an hour regardless of what I tell them."

"Okay. You are just now answering."

"Yes? Sario?" Clint "answered."

"Mr. Faraday, I have brought Sr. Penceros in, as was requested by the junta. I thought you were to be here to question him?

"There are two officers from the fiscalia here who wish to transport him to David. I must seek your permission?"

"I'll be there in forty five minutes. I'll decide whether or not they can move him after I ask a question or two.

"No. They cannot move him now."

"Er, Mr. Faraday? I'm Capitan Arnaldo Nuñez of the fiscalia in David. We would feel that it is more secure to take Sr. Penceros into David City. There are facilities where you can question him there."

"Denied. I have enough experience with the Chiriqui Fiscalia to know all I'd get there would be obstruction. The official corruption, such as we're investigating where Penceros is concerned, is rampant and obvious. This has already gotten past the point of excess bureaucracy. What I want from Penceros is simple. It shouldn't take more than five minutes, then you can take him.

"The longer you waste time arguing the longer before you can take him."

"Yes. We will expect you in forty five minutes, then," Sario said, and hung up.

Clint got out of the disguise. He put the cash in the safe in the trunk of his car along with the clothes, then put on his regular work pants and tee shirt. And sandals.

He drove to Chiriqui, getting there in half an hour. He wanted to surprise Capitan Nuñez and associate. He wanted to see what other pressure was brought to move Penceros – and by whom.

He went in the side entrance and directly to Sario's office. Nuñez and Lt. Dorcas were in the cell area talking to Penceros. He caught Sario's eye when the others had their backs to him. Sario soon came into the office.

"How far have they gone?" Clint asked.

"The cops? They say they're taking him into David at eight thirty two whether I like it or not. That is forty five minutes from when you said forty five minutes.

"What's Penceros' reaction to that?"

"I think he's what you might call 'terrified out of his skull' by the idea. He knows damned well he would never live to reach that facility.

"Clint, they don't know about the listening space behind that wall."

Clint nodded. He was shown a narrow hallway. Sario said to stand by the spot where the little white mark was on the stud. He went into the room to tell them he had some forms to file and would be in his office. He would come back as soon as Mr. Faraday came. If they didn't follow the orders issued by Mr. Faraday they would find themselves under intense investigation by the junta, given authority directly from the president.

Lt. Dorcas watched from the door until Sario was in his office, then slipped back into the interrogation cell. "He's in his office. What in Hell are we to do now? Faraday really is the authorized head of the board and he really does have the authorization that makes him superior to us!"

"We can say he said forty five minutes. He won't be here. He'll be stopped at any of three locations and asked for confirmation of orders. That will take half an hour and we'll be gone," Nuñez replied. "Penceros, we'll take you to the terminal. They won't expect that. You catch the Rio Sereno bus and walk into Costa Rica. Santos will be expecting you and will stamp your passport. Faraday has no authority for Costa Rica and can't make them send you back. This will be over in less than the ninety days even if we would let them send you back too early.

"I don't like being put in this position! I can see why Faraday hates us! Now we're stuck by the same shit! I just hope Felix can keep our heads off the chopping block!

"That shouldn't be a real problem. He can make Errends issue any order he wants. Penceros won't be available and there isn't sufficient evidence without him. Case is dismissed.

"Penceros, if anyone asks you about anything, you're deaf and blind and stupid and don't know anything. Costa Rica or here. Clear?"

"Clear. I really don't know anything."

"You know who the contact is here."

"So do they. Mancinni."

"Really? I sorta wish they would be able to get that bastard's ass! He's a damned fucking snake! You can't believe anything he says. If Felix didn't protect him, he would be dead ten years!

"I wonder what he has on Felix. It must be something really big!"

Nice to know! I'd like to know what he has on Felix, myself! Clint thought.

"Well, all we can do now is wait. When Faraday doesn't show we're home free!"

Clint waited until forty three minutes to go to let them get more and more nervous. No one will have reported that he was stopped anywhere.

He went to stick his head into Sario's office and grin. Sario got up from the desk and went with Clint to the room, where they were just standing to go.

"I'm in a hurry," Clint snapped. "One question.

"Laura or Yolanda or both?"

Penceros missed the chair and sat on the floor. Hard. Nuñez and Dorcas were staring at Clint with their mouths hanging open.

"It's an easy question. That you have the answer is shown by your reaction. Your fat ass will be one big bruise from that.

"Well?"

"I don't know. You already know as much as me. You mean all this was over that?"

"It also showed us a couple more cruds who are involved in the corruption.

"Sario, you have complete ID on these?"

"Yes, sir, Mr. Faraday."

"Then we can all go home. I'm tired. I'd wish you a good night, but know damned fucking well you won't have one! Except Sario. The board thanks you for your help in this matter."

Clint walked out. Sario muttered, for Nuñez et others to note, "Like I had a choice! You didn't get anything from me!"

"He didn't?" Dorcas asked.

"I did what his orders said I have to do. That didn't include volunteering anything."

That was carried to Clint through the cell phone in Sario's pocket. He grinned as the signal was cut off.

Sario just might collect a lot more evidence of corruption if they thought Sario was corruptible.

He waited until Penceros and the cops drove away and went back to the office.

"Anything more?"

"Not really. A little confirmation of what we already knew. You can listen to it."

"I can?"

He pointed to the sign as you come into the door.
This is a police facility.
Everything said here is recorded except in

"They're police. They should have known that before they said anything."

He turned to his computer and to the recording program. He had said he simply followed the orders Clint carried. He said there was no order to volunteer anything and there couldn't be. He didn't ever say he hadn't volunteered anything. Nuñez was the one giving orders from that group. He got a little cozier with Sario when Sario said there were a lot of people who would resent some gringo coming in and giving orders. Not much else was anything they could use on their case. It was a lot of things that the corruption board could use – if they would. Clint doubted very seriously that anything would be done beyond what he and Sario could force to be done. That would be with their case only.

Clint would handle that part tomorrow. He really was tired.

"Clint? Can you come to the judicial?" Sario asked on the phone at seven the next morning.

"Something up?"

"It could be. Somebody tried to kill DelaCruz."

"*DelaCruz?!*"

"Yeah."

"How? When? What?"

"Somebody shot him as he left the restaurant early this morning. He spent the night in his quarters there. He was wounded, but not seriously."

"Why are you even there? It was nowhere near Chiriqui!"

"Nuñez said it was connected to you, that you might have shot him because you couldn't get enough evidence against him to prosecute. He told them you as much as said that in my station and apparently thought I'd back him up.

"I brought all the recordings of when you were there so he could prove it.

"I'm a bit afraid to leave. Those recordings really have his ass in a sling, as you gringos say."

"I'll be there in fifteen minutes. Entertain them until I walk ... Sario, check where Beegee is!"

"Beegee? ... Oh! Why?"

"He missed. A professional wouldn't. He's getting a rep for missing. Me, now Felix.

"You know something? I think, just maybe, Felix will be our top witness!"

"DelaCruz? Why?"

"Because he has the goods on them. Trying to have him hit makes it better to give their asses to us than to let them kill him because he wouldn't. Their blackmail or whatever is probably better than getting knocked over."

"You have a point. I think I can entertain our

people here. If they try to hit someone as big as Felix, what is their sordid little life worth?

"This might turn into rather dangerous fun!"

"Don't ever forget the 'dangerous' part of that. Twenty minutes!"

He rang off and headed for his car. He was in the little restaurant near the hotel. He paid and ran. He was in the fiscalia well within the twenty minutes and charged into the room where Nuñez, Dorcas, a woman Clint had met from the PTJ, Penceros and Sario were sitting around a table drinking coffee.

"Hi, Bonita! Sario brought you in on this?"

"I did. She's the only one here I'm positive isn't corrupt. She tied my ass in granny knots a couple of times before and it was pure Hell getting the charges dropped. That's how Felix got me into it.

"Sario says he thinks he knows who tried to knock off Felix."

"Yeah. He misses more than he hits, pun intended. He missed me and didn't show a lot of accuracy with Felix. You all know who hired him."

"Mancinni," Penceros said, acidly.

"Probably. It's about his speed, but under whose orders? He didn't take this one from Felix you can be damned sure!"

"Both of them," Penceros said. "They have to get

rid of all of us. I'm ready to give a statement. It's going to be a fucking Hell of a lot more than they ever knew I know!"

Bonita was called to the phone. She came back in to say that everyone in the whole place was to take orders from Clint Faraday until their team from the junta headquarters arrived by helicopter in an hour and a quarter, in which case Almirante Quintero is in charge – with orders to collaborate as much as possible with Clint Faraday.

"What the hell is that about?" Clint demanded. "I don't want to be in charge of anything! This is ridiculous!"

"Bonita! TVN!" came down the hall.

Bonita turned on the TV and found TVN.

"... it on myself to aid in any way we can. It is the duty of the press to expose this kind of thing whenever we can. We have a duty to protect the public and the institutions ... make that the *legitimate* institutions ... of the people's government and of the people's courts. Even if that means protecting the people *from* those institutions!

"We have learned through confidential sources that Clint Faraday, who I am proud to call a personal friend, has started an investigation of the execution of a man, Ernesto Barco, who was exposing corruption in the aduana and border police. That has led to layer upon sickening layer of corruption. They have even resorted to murder in the case of Sr. Barco! It is beyond outrage!

"I knew nothing of this until a relative of the slain hero, Ernesto Barco, pleaded with me to investigate on my own. He was aware I am a personal friend of Mr. Faraday. Clint.

"I have tried to not interfere with Clint's work. I have been here on the sidelines taking notes, recording evidence.

"My experience with Clint makes me able to predict that there will be numerous arrests before this day is done.

"Back to you, Sandra."

"Thank you, Sonya. We will now take you to Juliana at the Ciudad Judicial."

"Personal friend? Well, I talked with her a few minutes when that purge thing was going on," Clint said.

A scene just outside. Juliana was standing with a microphone beside Judge Arenas.

"This is the Honorable (smirk) Judge Amelia Arenas of the circuit court.

"Judge, it is rumored that you are at this moment under investigation in this matter that is in session inside that very building, that you have taken bribes to close cases for lack of evidence when there was more than sufficient evidence, even prima facie proof. There are charges you are part of the clique with such as Guerra, who this station has shown to be less than forthright in his decisions, take as example the way he and his fellow ... crooks... were backed down by Clint Faraday, who is in charge of the session inside.

"How do you answer?"

"Answer what? All you did was make a series of malicious charges directed at others!"

"Perhaps. How do you answer to the charge that you have accepted bribes to close cases with more than sufficient merit?"

"I will not answer such ridiculous rumors. I will not elevate them into serious consideration."

"Uh-huh. In other words, the traditional 'No comment?' That's your answer?"

"I will not dignify such spurious *rumors* with reply!"

"No comment. Back to you, Sandra."

"We have just this moment received notice that a panel from Panamá City is en route, flying by helicopter to investigate charges that will be brought in Panamá City against a number of people. Those charges will range from public corruption to murder.

"Well, Tomas! It seems the famous Clint Faraday has upset another hornets' nest! Will the weather forecast bode good fortune to Clint's little escapade?"

"He's in David. Partly cloudy in the afternoon hours with some rain around sunset becoming heavier as the night progresses. Warm, but with a breeze. It will be a very good day for Clint – and a bad night for his quarry! In Bocas del Toro, we can expect..." Bonita turned it off.

"You're getting to be a pain in the ass, Clint! The rest of us aren't even here!"

Clint gave her the finger. "You aren't nearly as sick of it as I am! All I wanted to do was get the ones who killed Ernesto Barco! Why in *Hell* can't you people just leave it at that? Why do you always drag me into some national thing? Shit!"

"Well, the panel will get here soon. They have publicity that means they can't bury quite all of it. I just wonder which one kept the press on it!"

Clint took the phone out and went through the long list of numbers, then called one.

"Juliana? Clint Faraday here. Who kept you people on this? Him or her?"

"The wife, but the son backed her up all the way. She said you would avenge her husband's murderers. I think you will."

"I'm not out to avenge anyone. I merely said I'd catch the killer. That led to finding who paid them to kill him. I hope it will finally be done by tonight."

"I have the go-ahead to keep pressure on the panel. This one, more than a goat or two are going down! Hard and public!"

"Keep up the good work."

"You, too!"

"I'm gonna get some breakfast until the panel gets here and goes through the publicity speech bit," Clint said. "That should be about four thirty or five?"

"If we're lucky. I'll go with you," Sario said.

They left the rest of the group there under Bonita's protection. Anyone there knew better than to mess with her. They'd be safe enough.

"We find that the two are escaped to Costa Rica. Sr. Mancinni has caved and has given us plenty to prosecute the women, Laura Nuestras and Yolanda Chirenas. They are convicted of soliciting murder by testimony confirmed by Nacio, so Costa Rica will return them here. Sr. Mancinni, the one who made the payment for the murder and Sr. Penceros, who was the carrier of the blood money to Mancinni, will be charged. Evidence presented here will certainly insure their incarceration for twelve years. Sr. DelaCruz was forced into his actions, *in this case*, through blackmail. He has been tendered immunity, *in this case*. Other lesser charges will be pending against certain of the police officers and members of the court.

"This is a formal filing of said charges. We wish to commend Clinton Faraday for yet another action in the public interest.

"If there is no further business, this panel is adjourned." Norte looked around the room, then banged his gavel and sat.

Clint and his little group got up and went for a late dinner at La Tipica. The panel session broke up at ten oh five. La Tipica is 24 hours.

Clint was going back to his wife and family in Cusapín in the morning. He would stay at a friend's place in Gualaca tonight.

"Well, I hope we meet again soon, but without murders or corruption or any of that crap," Sario said. "Enough is too much!

"It was interesting, though. I sort of missed the investigation bit here. Now I go back to Chiriqui and a couple of overnight drunks in the jail and a stolen camera or laptop or bicycle to be my greatest excitement.

"I think I look forward to that!"

"I'm getting too old for this crap anymore," Clint said. "Give me the comarca and my wife and kids and digging yuca or fishing over murder anytime. The next one that comes up, tell your fellow cops about. Not me."

"You'd go crazy – if we would have a way to know – in a few months or less, without the investigations to keep you active," Bonita argued. "Face reality. It's what you were born to do!"

"I like it when Clint prods me into doing my job," Juliana said. "I've investigated fifty cases of corruption, had the goods and evidence, then that bunch threw it out as insufficient or something. With Clint, they don't dare!"

"We just thank God there is a person like Clint to help people," Sra. Barco said. "He says he does not believe, but he does God's work daily."

"He's a decent human being. There are less and less of us," Berto said.

"If you're going to get into this crap, I'm out of here!" Clint cried. "As Bonita says, it's what I was born to do so I do it. That's all!"

They chatted awhile, then went home and to bed.

"Clint! Phone!" Tyna called.

Cling wiped his hands and took the satellite cell phone from her.

"Clint? Sario here. Just wanted to tell you that it went pretty much exactly like the panel said it would. Nuestras and Chirenas were sent back in shackles from Costa Rica and got fifteen years apiece. When they get out there will be charges for murder. The fifteen years is for the corruption part. There's no limitation on charges of murder.

"So! How are you and the beautiful wife?"

"We're living in paradise. You gotta ask?

"How about *your* new family? Things going along smoothly?"

"Yes. We're happier than anyone has a right to be.

"DelaCruz has spoken with me several times. He sees what a dead end the crime business is and will run the restaurant and his legitimate businesses. He says what happened to Mancinni and the two women showed him that no one's immune from the inevitable end. He's stopped expecting it could be.

"You're quite the example, Clint Faraday!"

"Yeah, but we can't figure the example of *what*!"

They chatted a few minutes, then Sario rang off. Clint handed the phone back to Tyna and went back to tilling the soil for the frijoles.

This was the last one! No more murders! He could live without the ... nah!

C. D. Moulton's works are available on most major outlets as printed or e-books. CD writes the CD Grimes, PI, mysteries, the Det. Lt. Nick Storie mysteries, the Clint Faraday mysteries, the Flight of the Maita science fiction series, books on orchid culture and many others of many types. Mystery, adventure, intrigue, science fiction, humor, fantasy, paranormal, mild erotica, and factual.

www.ingramcontent.com/pod-product-compliance
Lightning Source LLC
Chambersburg PA
CBHW072206150726
48002CB00014B/1427